# DISTRICT ⑬

# LINE UP

**Alex Kuskowski**

**SADDLEBACK**
EDUCATIONAL PUBLISHING

# DISTRICT ⒀

Before the Snap

Down and Out

Fighting the Legend

The Handoff

Hit Just Right

**Line Up**

No Easy Race

A Second Shot

Taking Control

Wings

SADDLEBACK™
EDUCATIONAL PUBLISHING
www.sdlback.com

ISBN-13: 978-1-61651-279-8
ISBN-10: 1-61651-279-2
eBook: 978-1-60291-949-5

Printed in Guangzhou, China
NOR/0713/CA21301251

17 16 15 14 13    3 4 5 6 7

**1**

"Daniel! Dan-*iel*. Wait for me!"

Daniel Stubbs ignored the voice. It was a bad day at Northeast High School. He didn't need anyone bothering him.

"Can't you wait? Mom said you should." It was his little sister Kiara. Daniel shrugged. His mom said something before school. He didn't listen.

"Anyway," his sister continued, "Jamal's with me. I thought you'd wait for *him*."

"What up, brother?" Jamal Harris was Daniel's best friend. They met in the first grade. Jamal gave his usual fist bump greeting.

"Nothing much. Surprised you're still talking to me. I'm probably a grade-A nerd now." Daniel kicked a pebble.

"What! Naw man. You showed up that windbag Mr. Murphy good in class today. Gave him a what for on his fact checking. Nobody's calling you a nerd. Hero, more like."

"Yeah. I heard about that! Mr. Murphy's nas-ty," Kiara told the two boys. Daniel shook his head. They talked about it in the middle school? Daniel sighed. He had a NERD sign on his forehead now.

"You're on top of school. You ready to take on sports? Join the track team with me?" Jamal asked.

"Dunno man." Daniel shifted. "After today? School stuff isn't for me. You know? I'm not like you."

Jamal laughed. "You showed up Mr. Murphy today. You can show me up in sprinting."

"Who's gonna show Jamal up? Can I be there when it happens?" A voice came from behind them.

Daniel saw long brown legs and a bright smile. It was Simone Wallace. She had snuck up on their group. Daniel's face got hot.

Simone was the prettiest girl Daniel knew. She was also the fastest. She won state in track last year. Her black hair was shiny. Even her skin glowed. He'd never said a word to her. She was a friend of Jamal's. They ran track together.

"Uh …" Daniel couldn't respond. Simone had heard about him correcting Mr. Murphy. She probably thought he was a nerd.

Jamal jumped in to save Daniel. "Just sayin' he should give track a chance. You tell him, Simone."

"You should come! I heard you laid it down on Mr. Murphy today. Good work! Try laying down track. I'm sure Jamal will be eating your dust." Simone smiled again.

Maybe track wouldn't be so bad. He mumbled, "I guess I could. Tomorrow. Give it a try."

"Great. Can't wait to see you. Gotta run!" Simone jogged off. Daniel watched in a daze.

**2**

Daniel waited. Jamal would tease him for sure. Jamal only said, "You'll come? You owe me a race then."

Daniel stared. Jamal gave him grief before. Two weeks ago Daniel said Simone was fine. As fine as Jamal's girl, Destiny. Jamal didn't let Daniel forget then. Now, not even a peep.

"Yeah. I'll be there," Daniel said.

"Catch ya on the flip side."

Jamal ran off. He left Daniel with his sister.

Kiara ran her mouth. "Daniel's got a crush!"

"Drop it, Kiara." Daniel was angry.

"Simone is too pretty! You see her long wavy hair? You're ugly!" Kiara tossed her braids. She pretended to be Simone.

"Kiara I mean it!" Daniel opened their front door.

Kiara sang, "Daniel and Si-mone sit-ting in a tree. K-I-S-S."

Daniel banged the door. "Would you SHUT UP!" It was louder than he meant.

Kiara burst into tears.

"No way to talk, boy!" said Daniel's Grandpa. He was in the kitchen. Oh no. Daniel was in trouble. Grandpa Stubbs would walk out. Daniel would get a smack upside the head.

His ma came out of the kitchen instead.

"Daniel! Don't yell at your sister!" His ma stormed. She wore her nurse's uniform. She had a double shift tonight.

"She was nagging me, Ma." She looked tired. She didn't need this.

"I did NOT raise my son to yell. Apologize."

Daniel didn't say anything.

"Fine. Leave. Come back when

you can." This was too much. Kiara had asked for it.

"FINE," Daniel yelled. He ran out the door. He sprinted down the street. He didn't hear the door slam.

Daniel ran. Then he got out of breath. He walked. He slowed down by the basketball courts. He saw people he knew. Someone called his name.

"Yo Dan! My man!" It was Tyrese.

"What's up Tyrese?" Daniel said slowly. Tyrese didn't talk to Daniel. Not anymore.

Tyrese was like a brother to Daniel. He was older. He was cool too. Daniel's first running shoes were from Tyrese.

Tyrese dropped out two years ago.

He said to "hang with his boys." Now they caused problems. Sometimes the cops came. Tyrese often ignored Daniel. It made Daniel mad.

Tyrese waved his hand. The others on the court saw. They came closer. Daniel got nervous.

"I heard Jamal ditched you. You'll be needing a new crew," Tyrese said. He bounced his basketball.

Daniel shifted. Daniel didn't know the new Tyrese. This Tyrese was different. Dangerous.

"Want to hang with us?" Tyrese's friends stood with him.

"I dunno." Daniel's brain raced. Did he want to hang?

Tyrese's ball stopped. "I give an invitation. You don't know?" Daniel

saw Tyrese's teeth. He was angry.
The guys moved around Daniel.

"I … I … I'll think about it. I
gotta get home." Daniel turned
around. He ran as fast as he could.
He heard Tyrese's laughter. He
wasn't happy. He was angry.

**3**

Daniel thought a lot. He was upset about Tyrese. He was distracted. At school he was jumpy. He couldn't sit in the cafeteria.

He went out to the basketball court. He practiced his jump shot. Line up the point with your elbow. Jump and … Swish! Just like Tyrese taught him. Daniel shook his head. He focused on the basket.

Line up. Jump. Swish!

Now that Daniel had grown it was easy. Easier for him than even Tyrese. Tyrese used to be the star. He ran Northeast High School basketball. So why'd he quit?

Line up.

Tyrese wanted Daniel to join his gang.

Jump.

Daniel heard things. Some of the old members went to jail. People got arrested in Daniel's neighborhood.

The ball hit the rim. It bounced away. Daniel turned to pick it up.

"Practicing your jump shot? I taught ya that," Tyrese said. He bounced the ball at Daniel. Hard.

"How about those red and white shoes? Man, you could fly in those."

Daniel bounced the ball back. He was angry. Was Tyrese trying to butter him up? "I grew out of those, Tyrese. It was a long time ago."

"Come on, Dan! I'm just talking about old times." Tyrese took a shot. Net ball.

"Yeah. Well, don't." Daniel grabbed the ball. He dribbled. He ignored Tyrese

"Look, Dan. I came on strong. Yesterday was tough for me. Got to be a man for the crew. Sorry I wasn't around this summer. I had stuff to take care of. Personal."

Daniel's dribbling slowed.

"You don't have to join our crew.

Only if you want. I thought you might need some buddies."

Daniel looked at Tyrese. "I want to be friends, Tyrese."

Tyrese smiled wide. "Great! You don't have to be tight with my crew. But I got a favor to ask you."

"What?" Daniel asked.

"I need to borrow your Grandpa's gun. Just for a minute. Show my crew a real Vietnam War gun."

Daniel wavered. "I don't …"

"Look, just for an hour? He won't even notice it's gone." Was Tyrese being honest? There had to be more to it than showing his boys a gun. But he'd never lied to Daniel before.

"Think on it," Tyrese said. He took one last shot. Then he walked away.

**4**

"BRRRRRRRING!" It was the end of the school day. Daniel slammed his locker. Time for track. He worried about Tyrese. Would he come looking for Daniel?

Should he loan Tyrese the gun? Tyrese had changed. Who knew what he really wanted with it? And Grandpa Stubbs would kill Daniel if he found out.

"Hey, you ready? I'm gonna kick your butt!" Jamal punched Daniel.

"At running?" Daniel smiled. He was glad to be distracted. "We know you ain't got no game."

"Woah! Look at the big man now. See how you feel later. When we get out on the track."

The track was in poor shape. This wasn't new. Everything at Northeast High fell apart. But Daniel saw kids having fun. They even goofed around. Practice could be fun. But they were serious about winning.

Daniel squinted. Was that Simone over there?

Jamal was talking, "Over there are the hurdles. Hey! You paying attention?"

"No. What?" Daniel asked.

"Those wooden things over there." Jamal waved his arm. "I told you not to try them. They're hard. You've got to be real good. Don't goof off on them. Coach'll kick you off the team."

Daniel watched the varsity team practicing hurdles. It didn't look hard. Daniel jumped over a trash can once. It was to win a race. Even Tyrese was impressed then.

"You try yet?" Daniel asked.

"Yeah. He fell flat on his face!" Destiny ran by. She laughed at Jamal. She was Jamal's girlfriend.

"I'm gonna make you pay!" Jamal sprinted. He caught up to Destiny.

Daniel was alone. He looked around. He didn't know what to do.

"Need a guide?" Simone asked.

Simone helped Daniel out a lot. He made mistakes. He learned to not sit between the 4-by-200 runs. He stopped to rest after 200 meters. Everyone else ran it three more times. He made more mistakes. Like sitting on the starting blocks to rest. He was embarrassed. Simone called his name. He forgot to worry.

Daniel was having fun. Simone was so nice. And hot. Daniel wanted to be more than friends with her.

Everyone on track was friendly. They included him. They ran with him. They showed him stretches. People wanted to talk to him. Especially after he raced Jamal.

The race was once around the

track. They forgot the hurdles were on the far side. Jamal ran around the hurdles. Daniel wanted to jump them. Hurdles are smaller than trash cans.

He cleared one. Then another. Then another. Line up. Jump. Clear. Just like basketball. But easier.

Jamal won. But it was okay. Daniel saw people watching them. He surprised them.

Jamal walked up. "Can you do that again? Bro, you'll be king of this track."

**5**

Daniel waved goodbye. He'd made a lot of new friends. He walked home.

He was tired. He was sore. But he had fun! Maybe Jamal was right. Jamal was always doing something good. Cool girlfriend. Good in school. He even got along with his parents. That kid had it all together. Joining track wasn't all bad.

He unlocked the door to his house. He ran into his Grandpa.

"Grandpa! What are you doing?"

The old man laughed. "Son, I *was* making my way outside. It ain't no thing though."

"Do you need help?" Daniel asked. Grandpa's leg was a problem. Not that he complained. Grandpa used a cane in secret.

"Naw. Why don't you just sit with me?" He cackled. "Like those darn kids who laze around. Ain't anyone ever getting a job here?"

Nobody hired kids from the neighborhood. Daniel kept his mouth shut. He respected his grandfather.

He watched Grandpa. He sat down slowly. Then he looked down

the street. The old man had seen a lot. He'd been to war. Maybe Daniel could ask for help. He wouldn't say Tyrese's name. He'd just ask for advice.

"Grandpa, I have a question," Daniel blurted out.

"Well go ahead and ask it, boy! Don't be wasting my time with fool statements."

"Did you ever have a friend? A good friend. Who asked you for something? When it wasn't yours?"

"All the time, boy. That ain't a friend you're talking about." Grandpa gave him the eye.

"It's stupid. Forget it." Grandpa wouldn't understand.

"Now, son. Listen here. This metal

in my leg?" Grandpa pointed to his knee. His scars were under his pants. When Daniel was little they scared him. "I got it helping my 'best friend' sneak out of camp. I knew it was a bad idea. But he was my buddy. Brothers in arms, you know? Then a bomb blew and cut me open. He wasn't my friend no more then. He ran away. He left me."

Daniel's mouth was open. *That's* how Grandpa got his limp? "Then what happened?"

Grandpa chuckled. "That's another story. But I got home in one piece. And I learned something. The friends you can trust ask for nothing. No favors. No gifts. Nothing but your time."

**6**

Daniel thought. Was his Grandpa right? Jamal was his friend. He never asked for anything. He wanted to hang, that was it. Tyrese had been that way, but now?

Daniel went back to the track every day. It made Jamal happy. Simone said hi in the hallways too!

Daniel worked on his hurdles alone. He practiced after school. In secret he used old trash cans. He didn't want to get in trouble.

One day Daniel was sprinting with Simone. He wasn't fast enough to beat her. Yet.

Jamal appeared. He was with a man. Daniel had seen the man before. He was the track coach.

Jamal called, "Hey, Daniel! This is Coach Simmons."

"Nice to meet you, son." Coach Simmons shook Daniel's hand. Daniel knew Coach Simmons. He was the math teacher at Northeast. Simmons's class was supposed to be hard. Jamal was in the class. He said it was fun too. Hard and fun didn't go together for Daniel. But that was before track.

"I heard about you. You ran hurdles the other day. Mind showing me?"

Daniel swallowed and nodded. This was a test. What if he failed? Could he stay?

He was sweating a lot. He wiped his hands on his shorts. Then he started to sprint. The hurdles came up fast. Line up. Jump. Clear. He went faster. He was doing better than ever. He smiled. He was on the last hurdle. Then he felt his foot snag. He stumbled and fell.

Daniel was humiliated. He wanted to cry. He had done so much better before. He brushed himself off. The coach came up. He waited to be kicked off the team.

The coach patted him on the back. "Good job, son! It was great except for the last one there. I'll give you some pointers. I want you to compete in the next meet. It's on Friday. Think you can do that?"

"Yes, Coach!" Daniel was really happy. He wasn't getting kicked off! He'd get to compete!

Daniel walked home. He was over the moon. He couldn't wait for Friday. He thought of what he learned. Coach Simmons gave him a lot of tips. He was thinking hard. He didn't see Tyrese coming.

"Yo, punk! Where you been? I told you to get back to me." Tyrese looked really angry. Daniel didn't answer.

"That track stuff is for losers. You should quit that. Doesn't change the fact you owe me."

"What?" Daniel was confused. "I thought it was a favor!"

"Not anymore. Worried about Grandpa? Or little Kiara? She walks home all alone now. Want them happy? Bring me that gun tomorrow night. 11 p.m. at the parking lot near the store. Got it?"

Tyrese gave a hard look. Daniel swallowed. Then he nodded.

What was he going to do now? Tyrese was clearly up to no good. But Daniel was afraid for his family.

**7**

Daniel was nervous. He didn't sleep that night. He couldn't pay attention in class. He got yelled at.

His thoughts buzzed. What would Tyrese do? What if Daniel didn't bring the gun? Could he protect Kiara? Grandpa Stubbs? His mom? He had to protect them.

He passed Simone in the hall.

She said hello. He pretended he didn't see her. He was too worried.

Daniel was great at practice. He used his feelings. It worked. He cleared the hurdles. Fast. Other kids watched. Some cheered him on.

Destiny saw him. "Someone call the fire department!" she yelled.

"Yeah, that kid's on fire," Jamal joked.

"Call him 'Blaze,'" a senior captain said.

"They'll need a lot a firefighters to stop him!" someone else said.

Coach Simmons walked over. "Good work, kid. Get some sleep. You'll need it for tomorrow."

Daniel snorted. Not likely.

"Great job, Blaze! Can't wait to

see you at the meet." Simone smiled. His knees felt funny. What if she smiled again? While he was running tomorrow? He might not make it.

He packed up. More people called him Blaze. It was funny. Daniel fit in. He didn't want that to change. What could he do?

Jamal and Daniel walked home.

"Daniel. Man, what's eating you? We been tight forever. Tell me. Is it school?"

Daniel said, "It's not school."

"Tell me, bro. I want to help."

Daniel wanted to. Jamal was his best friend. He knew Jamal. He wouldn't rat.

"It's Tyrese." Daniel told Jamal the rest. The gang. The threats. The gun.

Jamal looked worried.

"Don't do it, man. Think of another way."

"Got to protect family. What about Kiara? Or Mom? Even you!" Daniel demanded.

Jamal grabbed Daniel's shoulder. "Look. Talk to my cousin. He's a cop. He'll know."

Daniel shrugged him off. "No. Too late, Jamal. I got to do this."

"Think about your family. Your friends. What if you get caught? You'll wind up in jail!"

"That's what I'm doing. Protecting my family and friends."

Daniel walked away. Jamal didn't say anything.

**8**

The house was dark. Daniel snuck downstairs. He unlocked Grandpa's gun case. It was wrong to take the gun. But like Grandpa said, "Family first." That's what Daniel was doing. Protecting his family.

He took the gun out of the case. It felt heavy in his hands. Wrong. The clock said 10:45. Daniel jumped. There wasn't time to think about right or wrong. He stuffed the gun in the back of his jeans. He left and quietly closed the door. Then he started running.

Daniel shivered. He was never out this late. It was cold. The streets were empty. Creepy.

Halfway there Daniel stopped. The bullets in the gun! He hid behind an empty building. He took out the gun. He removed the bullets. Just like Grandpa taught him. He put the bullets in his pocket. He started to run again.

Daniel slowed to a walk. The parking lot came into view. He could see Tyrese pacing. Daniel was afraid. He wished he were in bed. Tyrese saw him.

"Where've you been, boy?" Tyrese yelled.

Daniel jumped.

"Where is it? You got it?" Tyrese's eyes looked scary. Daniel couldn't see the whites. He backed away.

"I don't know Tyrese ..." Daniel stalled. Could he go through with it?

Tyrese went crazy. He was yelling and waving his arms.

"You don't know!? Look here, punk. You're gonna gimme the gun. We're gonna rob that store."

Daniel's eyes widened. "But ... But ... I can't. "

"You can," Tyrese snarled. "You can ... and you will."

Daniel looked down. Tyrese had a knife. It was pointed it right at him.

**9**

"I … I … It's in my back pocket,"
Daniel stammered.

"Get it out fool! Give it to me.
Start walking to the corner store."
Tyrese pointed at the empty store.

Daniel put his hand on the gun.
Should he point it at Tyrese? Would
it help? Daniel was nervous. Jamal
was right. Maybe he would end up in
jail.

Tyrese saw Daniel stop. Tyrese's eyes got bigger. Then he came at Daniel.

Daniel took the gun out. There was nothing else to do.

Tyrese's hand reached for the gun. Daniel pulled the trigger. Nothing happened. He remembered. He took out the bullets! He didn't want to kill anyone. Tyrese was yelling. Daniel heard sirens.

Daniel quickly put the gun back in his waistband. He had to get out of there. Now.

Tyrese knew what happened. He got even angrier. "Don't you run away from me. Boy! You shot at me!"

Daniel saw flashing lights. If he didn't run the police would get him.

"Sorry, Tyrese. I'm not going to help you," Daniel said.

"We're not done!" Tyrese yelled. "We're still gonna do this!"

Tyrese had lost it. Those cops were already coming. Daniel turned. He ran as fast as he could. Tyrese followed him.

Daniel ran better than at practice. It almost wasn't enough. The lights were right behind him. So was Tyrese.

Daniel jumped over a fence. Then a bush. Then a trash can. His feet were on fire. His lungs were on fire too.

He reached home without being stopped. He looked back. The lights and Tyrese's yells were gone.

Daniel snuck inside. He put the gun back.

He got to his room. He lay on his bed. His heart still beat fast. His thoughts flew.

What would happen now? Would Tyrese come after him? Could he protect the people he loved?

Daniel thought about Jamal. Daniel would talk to Jamal's cousin.

Tomorrow was the track meet too! Would he impress Simone? He liked her. What if Tyrese showed up? What if he hurt people?

Daniel was so worried. His mind was racing. It took a long time to fall asleep. And none of his questions had answers.

**10**

Daniel stumbled downstairs. He was tired and sore.

"You don't look good," Kiara told him at the breakfast table.

"Yeah, honey. You sure you want to race?" His mom was worried.

"I'm fine," Daniel muttered. He kept eating. "Just be there at three o'clock, okay?"

"We'll be there with our blow horns, kid." Grandpa Stubbs grinned.

Daniel grinned back. Grandpa always knew what to say.

He'd know where his family was. It would help to keep them safe.

At school people patted Daniel on the back. People called, "Good Luck! Run 'em into the ground, Blaze!" Daniel jumped at every noise. He was sure Tyrese was there. Waiting

"Yo! Daniel! Blaze! You hear the news?" Jamal asked. They were walking to the meet.

"What?" Daniel was nervous. He felt sick. Where was Tyrese?

"Tyrese is gone, man! My cousin arrested him last night. He got charged with drug possession."

"What!" Daniel said. He was shocked.

"Sorry, bro. I knew he used to be a friend. My cuz says he's going away. Won't be back for a long time. Tyrese didn't even remember getting arrested. He was that high."

Daniel felt light. His family was safe! Tyrese wasn't waiting! His whole day brightened up.

At the meet, Daniel walked onto the track. There was Ma and Kiara. Even Grandpa Stubbs was in the bleachers. A banner read, "Watch out! Blaze is coming for YOU!"

Could his day get any better?

"Hey Daniel." Simone came up to him. She seemed shy. Daniel wondered what was up.

"I wanted to give you this. For luck." Simone kissed Daniel on the cheek.

Daniel was too shocked to move. He watched her run away.

"Damn, boy!" Jamal whooped. "You got yourself a girl!"

Daniel was on top of the world. He grinned. He knew he'd run fast. Faster than he did last night. He wasn't even nervous about the race. He had luck on his side.

"Yeah. I think I do."